BARDO

A Novella

Joseph Edwin Haeger

Bardo
Copyright © 2023 Joseph Edwin Haeger
All rights reserved.

No part of this publication may be reproduced, distributed, or transmitted in any form or by any means, including photocopying, recording, or other electronic or mechanical methods, without the prior written permission of the publisher, except in brief quotations embodied in critical reviews, citations, and literary journals for noncommercial uses permitted by copyright law.

This is a work of fiction. Names, characters, businesses, places, events, locales, and incidents are either the products of the author's imagination or used in a fictitious manner. Any resemblance to actual persons, living or dead, or actual events is purely coincidental.

ISBN-13: 979-8-9861105-7-8
Cover art and design by Angelo Maneage
Edited by Kat Giordano
Printed in the U.S.A.

For more titles and inquiries, please visit:
www.thirtywestph.com

To all my friends: Forever rage in our hearts

"That's right, honey, he's dead, the pigs ran right over him."

—Roberto Bolaño, *Antwerp*

Bardo

18

They told me he wasn't going to be able to see through the glass. That it was a two-way mirror and there were multiple mirrors in the death room, so even if he knew there was an audience, he wouldn't know which mirror to look into. They didn't call it the death room, no—they used a much more sterile term, one I forgot the moment the words dissipated in the air. What was the point of neutering a name? Call it what it was: the death room. He looked right at us. He put a little bug in our ears, and while it all should have been over after he was gone, it wasn't. He didn't let it be. His words rang in the caverns of my eardrums, ricocheting and echoing deeper and deeper into my mind to the point where the synapses firing only fired those words. Nothing else penetrated my focus. I had to search. And I wasn't even sure if I was looking for fantasy or for reality.

26

"What if we didn't get him? What if an innocent man was put to death?" ... "He wasn't innocent" ... "But what if he didn't kill our son?"

7

My dad used to take me hunting. I learned how to handle a gun and track animals, but at a certain point I lost interest in stalking the woods for game. I started listening to the CDs my parents didn't approve of and driving country roads for the luck of coming across deer grazing next to a barbed wire fence. They still spooked but weren't as alert as they would have been deep in the trees. They were used to the rumble and clatter of cars passing them by all day long, so one slowing down was soothing to their ears. I'd upgraded from a bolt-action to a semi-automatic, and Cody had upgraded to a miniDV video camera. He was able to zoom in. The closer he zoomed in the grainier the picture got, but you still saw the limb disconnecting as the doe tried to run away. It's too bad it was on the other side of the barbed wire.

1

If he was going to be as dangerous as she made him sound, I wasn't going to be able to go in with a mini bat. I was going to need something better. More reliable. I was going to need a gun or something. A rifle or shotgun was too big and would shout my plans when a whisper was already too loud. They'd have plenty of time to arm themselves if they saw someone walking up to their front door with a gun like that. Really, all they'd have to do is shoot me on the porch, hide their drugs, and call the cops. They wouldn't even have to stage my body to make it look like self-defense because it would have been self-defense. And my name would be tied to the rifle clasped in my cold, dead hands. No, I needed a better angle. I needed a gun with no marks—is that what they call it? A clean gun. One that can't be traced. You need to know criminals to get connections like that and good thing for me, I was about to meet some criminals.

33

I couldn't bring myself to say how. I didn't trust myself in the moment to say it. I didn't even want to say his name in their presence. They didn't deserve to hear his father speak his name. I needed his picture to say it all for me.

37

The dew clung to the toes of my shoes. I should've kept an eye on the windows, but none of the people inside knew my intentions. I was afraid the gate made too much noise with its old aluminum hinges. I needed to remind myself, no one knew my intentions. The concrete steps made no noise when I walked up them. The door was heavy and the sound dampened from my knocking fist to the innards of the house. The footfalls on the other side fluttered across the tile—but I wonder if I would have retroactively changed the memory to lumbering thumps had a man answered the door? I held up the photo of my son. I should have been looking at her face, searching for visual cues that she was lying. I should have been watching. "Never seen him" … "Thanks." I pocketed the photo and collected more dew on my shoes as I walked back to my car. The small amount of moisture wasn't going to be enough to resurrect the dead yard.

4

It was dumb. A hole I didn't see, and when my foot went in, I overreacted. One of those things that shouldn't have been a big deal but ended up being a broken ankle. The pain was crippling. I tried to stand on it, my hand balancing my body with the help of a tree. Even my skull throbbed. When I tried to take a step, my body collapsed on top of itself. My dad crouched down, getting close to my face. "I'm not always going to be here. I can't carry you out of every situation. Some days you gotta look around, assess, and man up. Ignore what's happening tomorrow or even an hour from now or even twenty minutes from now. Focus on what's going to happen with that next step. Figure out the next step. Don't think about the hospital or the doctor. That's the future. The next step is now, and that's what you need to come to terms with. The pain ain't going away and no one is coming to help. It's up to you to come to terms with the situation. Right now, I can help, but I can't carry you." I'll never forget this moment. My dad died a few months later.

45

"And if you find him?" ... "I'll kill him" ... "Will that help?" ... "Yes" ... "Why? It's not going to bring him back" ... "It doesn't matter" ... "It might matter" ... "It doesn't."

21

Time is supposed to heal all wounds. The average time spent on death row in Texas is about ten years. I wasn't sure I was going to be able to last that long. Justice was what justice is, and I needed it sooner rather than later. Our lawyer told us with this specific case, the appeal process, and the facts at hand, we were lucky for the whole thing to go relatively quickly. Ness felt vindicated knowing he'd be dead in a few years. I spent the time in a purgatory, not able to move on until justice—an eye for an eye—was laid down. I couldn't heal or move on until it was an impossibility for my son's murderer to move on. A few years I could bear because I had to. Of course it wasn't easy, but nothing was now.

13

Sea-foam green. Something out of a movie set in the sixties. Or made in the sixties. Hell, I don't even know what's what anymore. I don't even like movies. The smiles were more like grimaces. They were warnings to turn back. To shake off the hands guiding me down the hall and waddle out of the place. Or fall on my side and work at the peeling paint on the ground until I pulled it up enough to roll my whole body underneath. Everyone knows they can only see you if you can see them, and if you're hidden in the floor there isn't anything that can hurt you. They'd walk in circles above you scratching their heads and searching in all the nooks and crannies, but they wouldn't think to look in the most obvious place—underneath their feet. They wouldn't think to look down and see the small lump forming beneath the sea-foam green paint, cracked and worn from years of feet fit into sandals marching to the executioner. The slippers didn't make any noise. I wanted to ask if this was the same room they used before the injections. Like, did they hang people in this room? Or electrocute them? Or line five men up with rifles, giving one gun the bullet and the rest blanks. Have them all shoot at the blindfolded man who may have stolen chickens or pigs or cows or something.

Blisters are like water balloons. Skin is elastic like the rubber, and an external force can push and pull and stretch it until liquid pours into the empty space. The more the skin is manipulated, the more it fills and the larger it grows. The skin is soggy and sags and waits to burst. The warm liquid dripping down and soaking into your socks. And if it's a long walk, blisters will form in the craters of previous blisters, waiting for their turn to rip and pop and ooze their acquired liquid down, from the folds of your skin to the folds of fabric.

16

We had our problems. Of course we had our problems. We were a family and all families have growing pains. Ness always wanted to give him a sibling, but I was never able to make the leap. I was too afraid of what was going to happen if we added another human into the equation. I was the good kid growing up and my older brother was the one who tested my parents. I never felt like I had the opportunity to push any boundaries. I needed to stay inside and in line so they could sleep easy—or sleep with only one eye open opposed to two. Early on I knew he was going to have issues with authority. He was going to have to do something to learn how it was done. He was going to have to inch right up to the edge, occasionally toeing over, or even diving onto the other side simply to know exactly how far it stretched and how far we were going to be stretched. My brother stretched me enough, and I didn't want to relive my childhood in the role of the parental figure. I didn't want to watch my son destroy his life like I watched my brother destroy his. If it was the three of us, I could put all my energy into him and make sure he got all the love and nurturing he needed. I wanted to keep an eye on him and make sure he turned into the conscientious member of society I was expected to produce. Empathy. I wanted to make sure I instilled that trait into his personality. But nature plays such a large role in the development of young minds. Christ, we could have had a dozen kids and I could have done everything differently and nothing would have changed. I should have. I wish I could get in a time machine to go back to give Ness every single thing she wanted because then maybe we'd be okay.

23

I waited until Ness fell asleep to turn the computer on and type in the street address. The house looked like any other. It'd been years since I opened the site. The trail was cold. It was static, and who knew if I was going to be able to find the signal? It was still there, according to the internet, so it was something. I don't know what I expected—dark clouds and the face of Satan hovering above it? Did I expect the sound of pained screams to rattle through my computer's speakers at the sight of the house? Objects were objects and they didn't absorb or sustain human emotions. They stayed. People were transient, and for all I knew, everyone connected to my son was long gone. I knew this, but at a visceral level, I hoped I knew wrong. I wanted something tangible I could hold up and blame for his death and then strike down. I wanted this house to pulse with the pain of his death. On one hand, I wanted it to feel bad so I could pity it—but on the other, I wanted it to be proud of taking his life. That way I could drive over with an ax and chop the bastard down—one chop after another, I could gouge away at the house. I could knock small holes into the walls until the small holes connected and made bigger holes, and the gaps would grow before the whole shit heap came crashing down. But no. It looked like any other house in this town.

41

Ness didn't want to believe his killer was still out there. She wanted to believe I didn't believe it either. For her it was easier to swallow the whole thing as a truth and do her best to get on with her life. For her, the worst thing already happened, and he had been avenged. The semblance of vengeance was better than the truth of vengeance. She slept at night.

24

My pillow cradled my head. Darkness looked down at me and I closed my eyes to it. I needed rest. Uninterrupted. And yet. The cracks between his sobs. It wasn't the crying or the begging. It was the negative space in between. The small silences amplified the tension, brimming and buzzing against the tiled walls of the death room. Without having a reason, I knew—primal, animalistic, in my bones—he was still out there. It was too late for the man getting injected. Nothing I said, no number of hunches, could reverse what was happening to him in that moment. Yet, he was kind enough to give me a parting gift. My son's killer was still alive.

The sheet on the padded mattress was soaked through. A stained ring outlined where the moisture ended and the clean edges began. No one wanted to come and change the bedding and after days of my sweat soaking further and further outward on the sheet I pulled it off myself. The mattress—vertical blue stripes running down the entirety of the padding with small buttons sewed on at what seemed to be random measurements—was starting to absorb my yellow sweat. Why was it yellow? Were toxins a sickly color? I always assumed they were going to come out gray, the same as filth off your body in the shower after a long day. That's what I assumed, but as usual, my assumptions were wrong. I was wrong, and no one wanted to hear about the epiphany I was having. It didn't matter if they were looking in my face—the moment I started talking, their eyes glazed over and they didn't care anymore.

56

"Is this about Frank?" ... "Give me your wallet" ... "And the girl?" ... "Wallet" ... "They had something to do with my son" ... "Wallet. Watch. Phone." ... "My son is dead" ... "Just give me your wallet."

35

Both the top and the bottom of the box were folded and tucked. Ness had told me if I taped the bottom it was going to be stronger and last longer, but it's not like we planned on pulling the box out every day, or even every week. At the time, I didn't want to walk upstairs to find the roll of packing tape. "It's a good idea" as I folded and tucked. The years were marked in ink on the outside of the Ziploc bags. The insides filled with Polaroids, 4x7s, 5x8s, and school photos. The last few years with just Ness and I were lighter than the rest. The box was heavy, but not heavy enough to stop me from pulling it out by myself. A family's life tucked into a laundry room corner. Years to be assembled and picked up in my two arms. An entire visual life confined to a single box. Inside the bags there were growing and changing bodies. Adding and subtracting people over the course of our lives. The world's styles, evolved or devolved, were documented on the glossy photographs. But now, he was stagnant. No more metamorphosis to take place. These photos were stone and he was set in them, for now and eternity. I thought the inside was going to smell musty, like an old folks' home. It didn't smell like anything but air. I pulled out a stack and flipped through them. Many were out of focus. Some had awkward framing. Some had the reflection of the flash bouncing off a mirror or window, obscuring the entire photograph. Some were okay. A few were good. The majority were worthless. Was this what every bag was going to be? Could his life be boiled down to a dozen photos, not enough weight to even notice? The strain I felt in my back from pulling the box out was for piles upon piles of nothingness. I picked my favorite photo from the three good ones. I could refold the box when I got home.

32

She said it like no one has ever made a mistake, as if the courts weren't fallible. Like no man was put to death for something he didn't do. She should know—she was there with me. She heard the timbre of his voice crack against the tiles. Nothing more than a caged animal looking destiny in the face. But some things were easier. Some paths were simpler.

58

Dust coated my mouth when I woke up. My nose was stuffed and felt broken. I must have mouth-breathed for the rest of the night. My car door was ajar. The morning was stiff and silent and cold. I pushed myself to a sitting position, which was enough to feel the muscles in my chest tighten and scream from the bruises forming. Under my leg I found the photo of him. It was covered in a thin coat of dust and it had a few new wrinkles, but his face was still legible. It was clear enough to use. I leaned over so I could reinsert the photograph into my back pocket. I got on my hands and knees and crawled to the car. I wasn't ready to stand. Sitting was making the rushing blood to my head excruciating. I lifted myself into the driver's seat. They had left me my car keys. I'm not sure what they would have done with the keys and not the car, but I wasn't discounting my blessings. I turned the ignition, but nothing happened. Not even a click. I turned it back to the off position and then tried again. Nothing. My head drooped forward. I pushed the headlight button back in. The center console had spare change, but I wasn't sure if it was going to be enough.

17

He was my son, and of course I loved him. There came a moment when we had to choose between giving in to him or implementing an even stricter rule. We chose the latter, and I don't think I'll ever stop wondering whether it was the right decision. Could grace have been the right path, or did it matter? Had we been more lenient, would I be sitting here wondering if he was dead because we were too easy on him?

10

A lesson I learned quickly in my youth was no one gave a shit what I said. No one cared to hear my side of the story, and the more I tried to tell them, the harder the punishment was going to be. When my lawyer told me I was going to be hanging out for decades to come, I figured it was going to be a simple case of keep my mouth shut and let them forget. I wasn't going to complain because I did do some bad things in my life. I was a guilty person, if not for the reasons they had me locked up. I didn't mind being locked up. No, because that was something I had come to expect after being the usual suspect wherever I went. School? Cut-out porn was shoved in my face by the vice principal because Jeremy Peterson thought it was going to be hilarious to tape that shit up in the boys' locker room. They never even questioned Jeremy Peterson. They pulled me, Todd, Cody, and Ron into the office and started shoving the chopped-up porn into our faces. We denied it, of course, but still got a five-day suspension and academic probation. I'm not saying the deck was stacked against us, but that happened in eighth grade and three of the four had dropped out by our junior year of high school. There was no point arguing with someone that had their mind made up. There was no point in trying to proclaim your innocence—even when you were innocent—because that was going to get you into deeper trouble for lying. For having the balls to think you could look an adult—an elder—in the eyes and tell them an untruth, even when it wasn't. Just the mention of your innocence made you more of a fuck-up. It made you guiltier, and the best thing you could do was steel yourself for the initial punishment they had in mind. Take the sentence like a man and move on.

70

"Not one of us is innocent. Layers of guilt. And now, you too."

29

When I got home, I walked into his room. It looked like it did when he was still living here. Before he moved out the first time. He had trophies from his little league teams lined up on the mantel above his bed. He wasn't the best player, but he could hold his own, fit in with the good teams. I admit he was a damn good chameleon, but you can't fake athletic talent. I stood at his bookshelf and started to stack books. The box at my feet was half full. "We can do this later." Ness leaned on the doorway. I pulled another book off the shelf and put it on the stack I was building. I slid the stack of five off and placed it in the box. The entire room needed dusting. He never liked doing his chores, especially dusting. The trophies didn't even look shiny anymore. The dust was so old it started to become another permanent layer on top of the cheap plastic.

38

Yes, I was grasping at straws, just like she said. But a fistful of straws was more than a fistful of nothing, and even if the information I had was hollow and didn't lead to anything, at least it started with a door to knock on. It had something for me to do and that's all I wanted. A direction to point my feet.

8

It was supposed to just be a release of aggression. A couple punches and I'd resume the tight circles, but after the pain ran through my knuckles and up my arms it was like quenching a thirst. I couldn't stop punching and screaming. Flakes of the cinder blocks fell to the concrete floor. I'm not sure when I broke my finger, but it's not what stopped me. The guards had to pin me down and sedate me.

52

I needed sleep. I needed to go home. I needed to hug her. I wanted to do those things, but I also needed to tell her what I did. She deserved to know. But she also deserved to stay in a state of ignorance. It really was bliss, and the moment I told her about his jagged broken teeth she'd know I'd changed the course of our life forever. Changed it again. Will she see it as a gift? Will she see it as my parting gift to her? Her not having to worry about leaving me or waiting until I die to move on with her life?

12

"Do you have anything to confess?" ... "I'm not Catholic" ... "Is that a confession?" ... "I don't think so" ... "That was a joke" ... "Oh, sorry" ... "You don't have to be. Being Catholic isn't a prerequisite for confessing one's sins" ... "I've done a lot of drugs" ... "Anything else?" ... "I've lied and stolen—even from people who loved me" ... "And you feel guilty about this?" ... "I feel bad about it, sure" ... "And the boy?" ... "I'm sorry he's dead."

25

The company offered bereavement pay. It was enough time to cover the funeral, but not much more than that. I wasn't able to take the months I needed to grieve. I didn't get to wallow under my sheets and wait for day to turn to night to turn to day to turn to night and lose track of the numbers on the calendar. I set my alarm every single day, not that I needed waking up. I drifted. It all drifted. I didn't take the bereavement. We cremated him during the week and had the memorial service on a Saturday.

51

I told her not to follow me down. I left the front door open behind me, so it was easy to hear her howl. I know the howl. When the cops came to our house Ness wailed and wailed. If you want to hear how primitive human beings are, present a parent with a dead child. The sound doesn't come out of the diaphragm or the throat or the mouth. It comes out of the air around you and shakes the world into a stuttering frozen frame. I did not wail or howl or cry. From the moment the cops started talking a numbness washed over my body and I was worthless to the world. I wasn't going to do another good thing in the span of my lifetime and I knew it. In that moment, I became an anchor for Ness and she was going to have to cut deep ties to get rid of me. She'd have to vanish in the middle of the night or I was going to lumber behind her waiting for my turn to die. That was going to be the best way for her to cut ties with me: my dying. I heard the woman when she found her dead meth head boyfriend, and it's clear her howl didn't quite match Ness's wail. I guess a lover falls lower than a child on the hierarchy of primal connections.

39

I didn't sleep. I sat in my car in our driveway waiting to build the courage to go in and lay down next to Ness. I could tell her I needed to take a drive to clear my head, but what was I going to say when she noticed my head wasn't clear? That it was as foggy as it had been since the moment the detectives came to our door? Now that the man was executed, the fog thickened and I tried to work on this new chore. I was treading water, but still inching closer to something. The imaginary conversation with Ness was exhausting enough in my head to keep me sitting in the car. A dull green light emitted from the dash. I stared at the numbers on the speedometer. I reclined my seat and shut my eyes, not that it mattered.

73

The cops put the cuffs on too tight. The metal pinched the thin skin on my wrists. I imagined the yellow bruise that was bound to sprout after they took them off, and the court was going to gaze upon the discoloration. Was this small temporary defect going to help them look at me fondly, like a fellow human being? Or was it going to be a reminder of what I'd done?

50

"Someone killed my son" ... "I don't know who you are." I showed her the picture. It was bent, but easy to see his face. "I was sad to hear about that" ... "Me too" ... "I would have thought" ... "Who did it?" ... "They got the guy who did it" ... "Someone else did it" ... "How do you know" ... "I just do" ... "Like intuition?" ... "Something like that" ... "What makes you think I know who did it?" ... "The guy downstairs was at the house earlier that day. What was he doing there?" ... "Probably selling or picking up" ... "Did he do any killing?" ... "Frank's not a killer—he's a sweetheart." ... "He didn't seem like it answering the door" ... "He's protective" ... "Who would he have been selling or picking up for?" ... "Pops, do you even know what you're doing?" ... "I'm winging it" ... "I've never been good at winging things" ... "Me either."

1

They told me these kinds of cases dragged out, and even once the verdict came in it was going to be years before I needed to think about marching down that hallway. They told me I was going to sit in a cell, reading books and daydreaming about freedom until I aged out and they stopped caring. A forgotten prisoner. It's cheaper to keep us alive anyway. But the whole thing seemed to get streamlined for God knows why. The lawyers said it was "an appeal from the family." An appeal to sympathy, and apparently the judge didn't understand the notion of blind justice. Our own appeal process was shot to shit before it even had a chance to take hold. I didn't even make it through one book, granted I'm not much of a reader and maybe I picked something a little long—thirteen hundred pages too long—but what was I expecting? A lifetime to finish the thing. More than a few years. The trial was on and done, and before I knew it my legs were shackled and rattling down that sea-foam green hallway. It all seemed to slip by without much effort, like a life wasn't on the line. I didn't get it, but guilty is as guilty does. The paint peeled up off the floor and the ceiling tiles drooped down, looking like the lopsided grins of the dead.

22

The police didn't offer the details, but they gave us information when we pressed. Weeks after they found his body, a manila envelope arrived in our mailbox. It was the police report with all the small details. Times, locations, and names. The names were all redacted and blacked out, and the paper was photocopied so I couldn't hold it up to the light at an angle to try and read the indentations from the ballpoint pen. The address was there, right at the top of the report. It could have been a mistake. Maybe it was supposed to be blacked out the same as the names. But it was there—mistake or not. The location my son was found for the last time. I recognized the street name, but couldn't visualize where the house was actually located in the city. I didn't have any bearing on the spot. I was going to have to go there.

47

It was in his room, on a mantel. I wiped the collected dust off of it and picked it up. It felt small in my hands. I bought it for him as a souvenir at a major league game. We drove five hours to get to Houston. Ness didn't want to go with us, so she dropped us off at the stadium and went somewhere to shop. There was a fly ball I tried to catch for him, but we didn't have gloves and the ball landed three rows above us. Late in the game we went to the concession stand and the gift shop caught his eye. We walked in and I told him he could get one thing. The miniature bat was the first and only item he picked up. He did the obligatory lap around the store, and then presented me with the bat. I paid and he clutched it for the remainder of the game. He was so excited to show his mom the new toy he got at the game. On the long drive home he fell asleep, the bat tucked into the folds of his arms on his lap. He put it up on the shelf when we got home, and I wonder when he finally forgot it was ever there. I hope it was before he got into drugs. I don't want the loss of that memory to be because of drugs. I hope it was regular adolescence.

55

The car took a moment to turn over, and the slow chugging in the middle of the night echoed against the mills. I flipped my headlights on, illuminating another man standing in front of my car. He was wearing dark pants and a leather jacket. A stocking cap pulled down to his eyebrows. "Sorry, I'll get going. This is all a—" shards of glass rained against the side of my face. Hands reached through the window and clasped around my arms. I pushed them away and began crawling to the passenger seat. The driver's side door opened and someone grabbed my ankles. The seats were old and saggy, but my grip slipped and I was pulled out onto the gravel.

68

We stared at each other for a long moment. He moved the toothpick around his mouth, gnawing on it with his molars. The gun hung down at my side, two bullets left. I pulled the photo of my son out from my back pocket. I tossed it toward the coffee table. It spun through the air between me and the man sitting on his couch. It didn't look like his heart rate had sped up at all. The photo of my son landed face-up on the glass next to the box of bullets. The man glanced at it, then looked back up at me. He chewed the toothpick a little slower.

34

I lifted the frame off the wall. It was one of the last photographs we had of him smiling. It was his senior picture. I moved it around in my hands. My fingers drummed the glass. Small swatches of dust collected on the prints of my fingers. I turned it over. There were small metal tabs holding the back in place. "Don't you dare." She didn't waste any more words. And her gaze drifted away from me as she disappeared down the hallway. I did my best to straighten the frame on the wall, but it kept drooping to the left.

48

"You fucking retarded? I told you to get your old ass off my motherfuck—"

59

The clerk at the counter gasped when I walked in. A dollar seventy-five jingled in my pocket. I needed a little to eat and then I'd start walking in the direction of the house. I didn't want to go in the morning anyway. I needed to wait until at least noon, but dusk was going to be the best time. "I'll be right back" I told the kid at the counter and I wandered down the hallway to the bathroom. Before I had a chance to pee, I caught a glimpse of myself in the mirror. Blood was caked and dried across the left side of my face. The final kick of the night busted my nose, and I saw two horizontal purple and red cracks to prove it. Watching my reflection in the mirror I brought my hand up and tried to feel the bridge of my nose, but the pain was acute and instant. I stifled a yell and moaned instead. I needed to pee. Then I could try to clean the blood around the pain. And then I could get my cheap breakfast sandwich. And then I could start walking.

36

I didn't want to tell Ness where I was going. She wanted to destroy the report, calling it a morbid keepsake. She was disappointed enough to hear that I'd gone to the house once already. I omitted the part about parking and getting out of the car, attempting to build enough courage to walk up the grassy walkway. I told her I slowed down while I drove by, so I could get the best look at the house without stopping.

28

"What makes you so sure he's still out there?" ... "What makes you so sure he's not?" ... "Jesus Christ, we've been over this. You're grasping at straws" ... "I don't have anything else to say, but when I get the guy, we'll be happy. We'll be in a better spot" ... "We're never going to be in a better spot" ... "Not when you think like that" ... "Our lives are changed forever" ... "Our life can still be fixed" ... "They're not broken like that."

5

They didn't even try. I was there. My prints on everything—the body, the weapon, all over the damn house—but I was passed out and unaware of what was happening, or at least I thought I was. I'd been picked up before and I know that didn't help me—the small and medium transgressions of my past. They said I was blacked out, but blacked out or not, you'd remember murder. You'd remember your hands gripping a knife, or a gun, or someone's throat. It's something that codes itself into your DNA. Muscle memory reverberating through your bones to remind you of what you did. But I was the one there. They had my proximity to the body and an anonymous call, because that didn't seem suspicious to anyone else. They didn't believe me when I said I didn't remember a thing. They thought I was faking, and based on the severity of the murder, well—I'm sure I've done things leading me further down this path, and I have to come to terms with that. All sin is equal in the eyes of the Lord, and now I have to be made an example. I have to be the symbol that jerking off is as bad as rape is as bad as saying "God damn it" is as bad as murdering a kid who was as high as I was is as bad as not believing.

42

I hadn't driven my car much since he left high school. During his first couple years at Central High I felt like a chauffeur. This was before his friends had driver's licenses. The days when he called me collect from the mall's pay phone and quickly said "we're ready, come get us" into the spot designated for the caller's name. We never paid a collect call bill. I declined them after I heard his plea to be picked up and grabbed my keys.

19

I wished I took Ness's advice and called a taxi to take us. My mind was numb—yes—but the level of disconnection transferred to my whole body. My hands felt too large for my surroundings. I gripped the steering wheel and inched the car through traffic. My foot too heavy in its dress shoe as I pushed hard on the brake pedal to make sure I wasn't letting it up. The last thing we needed was to pull off to the side of the road because of an easily avoidable fender bender. How often did the brake pedals snap off under the weight of a driver's foot? Has it ever happened? I mean, nothing is an impossibility, and cars are man-made machines, so having a pedal break had to be inevitable. If I called one of the major manufacturers, would they tell me the statistic for broken pedals, or would they pretend like it's something that hadn't ever happened? Or no one had ever reported it? I needed to call a mechanic. They didn't have any reason to try and hide the truth to protect a facade of complete safety. They didn't have to convince anyone that owning and driving a car was the safest thing you could do. There's nothing safer or more attractive than driving a car, so don't worry about the brake pedal snapping off in the middle of freeway traffic where your car could possibly careen into the car in front of you. That won't ever happen if you own a car. I pushed harder on the brake pedal to make sure I didn't inch too close to the car in front of us. I didn't want to bump him. That was the last thing we needed.

Opening my eyes, I expected to see smoke drifting around the room, but it was as clear as it had been twenty seconds before I fired the gun. The carpet was stiff. The shock of the loud blast didn't affect the floor, or really any of the inanimate objects in the room. Except the wall. The short guy laid face down in a pile of his own brains. They seeped out like a hose moments after you turned the spigot off. The spray on the wall was thin, like the bullet created a mist that floated in the air for a moment before drifting onto the egg-white paint. I turned my body. I was lucky enough to hit one of the guys in the throat. His hands lay limp on his chest, like he tried to stop the flow from the wound but didn't realize he was bleeding out of the back of his neck too. There was a short blood trail, and the third man's feet stuck out from around a corner. "You good, Leon?" ... "Fuck no! Motherfucker shot me in the gut" his legs shook when he yelled. "Can you put the gun down?" I turned to face the man on the couch. "No" ... "Fair enough, but how about we don't shoot any more people?"

30

I wasn't going to sleep. I was going to sit at the edge of my bed and let my mind wander. Ness wanted me to lay down next to her, but whenever my head hit the pillow it started to hurt. A headache wormed its way deeper and deeper, and then I began to think maybe an actual parasite was burrowing itself into my brain, but at a certain point the deeper I imagined the worm digging the more I realized I didn't have that much brain. My body had finite capacity, and if I followed the imaginary worm all the way down through my skull, it was plausible there was nothing there but me.

3

It was essentially solitary confinement. Legally they had to let me go outside for an hour a day, but the guard glanced at his watch after about twenty minutes and shuffled me back inside, no different than cattle. A one-man herd. The cracks ran along the walls like veins in a forgotten giant. The hollowed capillaries dry from years of dismissal. I walked circles in my cell. My fingertips ran along the grain imprints, looking for the knots in the wood. Small changes in each board, but it all felt like crumbling, aged concrete. How many others had done the same thing? I only know my own mind, although I have to imagine more men than me have done it, but not all men are like me and I'm not like most men. I could have been the first to walk the tight circle.

27

The house where it happened was on a corner. The sidewalk was cracked and broken. A section rose above the others, pushed from beneath by a tree root. The house looked like any other on the block except for the browning yard. Did the house look the same when he was here? There was a sprinkler sitting in the center of the dead grass, the hose disappearing around the back of the house, but it didn't seem to have ever been turned on. Long vinyl blinds blocked every window of the house. It looked worse in person, but not by much. The house itself didn't embody the pain I wanted it to. It didn't take on the malicious nature I needed it to in order to blame it—to point my finger and say, *You're the reason my son isn't here right now*. Maybe it was how I felt about being this close to the house. I didn't bother opening the gate and walking up to the front door. I didn't have anything to say. I would have been a stranger on the stoop with no questions brimming on the tip of my tongue.

54

Someone tapped on my window. My eyes opened a crack, but a bright light made me shut them again. The tapping continued, sounding hollow from the interior of the car. Muffled talking. I didn't care to ask for clarification. It could've been neighbors, but in the middle of the industrial area there were no residential spaces. There weren't any houses out there—the precise reason I chose to park next to the big, empty mills and catch a few moments of shut eye. The tapping sped up and got louder. I squinted, looking at my dash. The clock read 4:04. I dug the keys out of my jacket pocket and I plugged them into the ignition. I put a hand up, waving to the knocker. "Sorry, sorry. I'll get out of here." It was probably the cops—flashlight in hand trying to get rid of a loiterer. Hopefully the woman didn't see my car. Hopefully she hadn't even called the cops. She was going to have to scrub the house down to circumvent any charges herself. She needed time and I needed time and this person tapping on the car window was in the middle of a misunderstanding. It was all a simple misunderstanding.

43

"Old man, get the fuck off my porch before I crack your motherfucking crown."

63

I wasn't sure if I was supposed to call ahead. If it was a faux pas to show up on a dealer's porch without an appointment. The door opened a crack and a young man stuck his face into the opening. He didn't say anything. "I need service" I stammered. "Fuck does that mean?" ... "I need to buy some stuff. I was told I could find it here" ... "Who told you that?" ... "Frank." The guy rolled his eyes. He shut the door and I heard the chain lock come free. He opened the door and stepped onto the porch. "Spread them" ... "Excuse me?" ... "Your legs. Spread them. Put your hands in the air. Got to pat you down before you go in." He felt up and down my legs, he shoved his hand into my crotch and the crack of my ass. He checked my armpits and torso. "Take your belt off and leave it on the porch." I followed his instructions, draping the leather belt Ness got me as an anniversary present across the back of a vinyl lawn chair. "If you're a cop we'll fucking kill you faster than you can say 'I need service.'"

9

When I was young my dad took me camping. My cousins came along and my dad gave me the choice: I could sleep in their tent with them or I could sleep in the bed of his pickup truck with him. I told him I wanted to sleep with him because the truck was metal and it was going to be safer if bears attacked. There wasn't a concern for my cousins sleeping fifteen feet away.

31

"You can rest. We got the guy" … "Maybe" … "There was a trial. We got him."

14

The straps were padded but still cut into my skin. They left the splint on my finger, as if it was going to matter within a few minutes. Where the wool made contact with my arms and legs, I wanted to scratch. I wanted to let them know there was a slight itch on the inside of my wrist, but they wouldn't have cared. Why care about someone moments away from not caring about anything, someone who was moments away from entering into nothing? I hoped for an afterlife, but everyone knows, deep down, when you die you cease to be—in the same way you ceased to be before you were born. What was it like before you were born? It doesn't even matter because it's all beside the point.

71

The gun felt more natural in my hand than the mini bat did. I leveled it at his chest. All I had to do was pull the trigger and it could be done. But his words echoed in my head and they bounced off the other words that had been bouncing around my head for the past week and there wasn't anything I could do about that. I'd have expected my hand to shake holding a gun, hesitating while the barrel stared down at a man. It could have been how calm and collected he was. It's not that he didn't think I was going to pull the trigger, because he saw how capable I was. And it's not that he had come to terms with his own mortality. His face told it all. He was calm because he didn't care what happened. If I shot him multiple times in the chest he was going to die and that was going to be the end of his life. If I dropped my arm and walked out the door, he was going to have to clean up my mess and that was going to be his next moment in life. It was like he had boiled it down to two outcomes: you live or you die, and then you deal with it. He breathed in deep and sighed. He didn't take his eyes off mine. He said what he wanted to say and I contemplated what I wanted to do next.

57

The tip of the boot hit me in the sternum. It knocked the air out of me and my body curled like a shrimp. He kicked again, harder and I balled myself tighter into myself. I felt hands all over me. They tugged my wallet out of my back pocket. "Can you leave my—" A kick to the face jerked my head back, and I felt a crick embed itself in the back of my neck. I was going to feel it in the morning. I was going to feel every single one of the kicks in the morning.

40

The gate made less noise, but the lawn looked deader in the daylight. The door wasn't as heavy. Nothing was the same at this time of the day. Almost a whole new house. The woman from before answered the door. She glanced down at the photo I had clutched in my fist. I didn't bother showing it to her. "I don't know…" … "He was my son and he's dead" … "I'm sorry to hear—" … "And it was here. He died here." She pulled a pack of cigarettes out of her bra and flicked one into her mouth. She closed the top of the box and was about to put the pack back when she locked eyes with me. She held the box out. I shook my head. She shrugged and tucked the pack back into her bra. Out of the other cup she pulled a lighter and lit the tip of her cigarette. "It's been a while" … "I know." She took a long drag off the cigarette. "Tony" she yelled it in one syllable. I showed Tony his picture. I was smart enough to watch his face this time. If he tried to deny anything, I'd know I had him. "I told the detectives, I wasn't here" … "You know who was?" He nodded. "Were they a friend of yours?" He nodded. "They both were" and he rubbed his eyes with the back of his hand. "Was there anyone else here?" … "Earlier" he looked up at me. "You know where I can find them?" … "It's been a long time since I've talked to them" … "Can you change that?" He gave a slight nod, almost small enough to not be noticed. I pocketed the photo and pulled a small notebook out of my other back pocket. "Got a name?" ... "Frank."

64

"What do you want?" ... "Um...angel dust, god powder, or whatever you call it" ... "I have no idea what you're asking for." I shuffled my feet and looked down. I hadn't taken my shoes off in two days. It was too forward to ask for guns at the start. A small amount of trust needed to be built before I asked this man to commit a felony offense. "You pat him down?" I felt the nods behind me. "Meth. Coke. Smack. Heroin. Blow. Cocaine. Pills. Pot. K. Weed. Whatever you want to call it, I guess—I've got most all of it" ... "Guns?" My mouth had moved before I thought about the word. He sat deeper into his couch. His arms spread out over the back of it. A toothpick, controlled by his tongue, moved around his mouth. "You don't want no drugs, do you?" I didn't feel my head shake. The world was going numb again. "T, grab the firepower. You know what you want?" ... "Something easy" ... "Ever shot a gun before?" ... "No" ... "Bring the snubs out."

53

The interior of my car got cold. I should've brought a blanket but didn't think I was going to be pulling into the industrial part of town to sleep in my sedan. Every hour I started the car and let it run for ten minutes until the heater warmed the cab, and then I'd turn it off for thirty minutes and try to keep my eyes closed. The nipping cold ate at the exterior of my body until I gave in and turned the ignition. The vents blew dust around the car. I couldn't get away from the dust. It collected and lay, hoping to become a permanent fixture. But it wasn't conscious—it didn't mind being swept into the garbage. Mostly because it was dust and didn't have the capacity for emotion. That was a dumb thought I had. I'm sorry. I'm sorry for it all.

44

I could make it back in time. It's not like meth heads slept all that much, or minded someone knocking on their door at 11 p.m. I mean, they clearly minded strangers knocking on their door, but it's not like they were asleep or busy doing something important. Round trip of an hour and I'd be back on the porch, more ready than I was. I even knew what I was going to take back to alleviate the fluttering beats of my heart. The picture was creased and wrinkled living in the back pocket of my jeans.

The shortest of the three men brought out a folded towel. He laid it on the coffee table and unfolded it with care. Pressed into the fabric were three guns. They all looked the same to me, except one was silver and the other two black. "Are they loaded?" ... "What do you think?" I looked at the man on the couch. He nodded his approval, and I picked up the silver one. It was heavier than I was expecting. The weight felt like it was distributed evenly through my hand, but I'd never held a gun before so I wasn't sure if it was how a gun was supposed to feel. As far as I knew, this was perfection. No one had ever held a more perfectly made gun before. I pushed on the cylinder with my thumb, but it didn't budge. I shifted my weight onto one leg and pressed harder with both thumbs. "There's a release button on the other side" he said it with a smile. He was watching a child learning to use their motor skills, one small step at a time. I moved the small latch and pushed the cylinder out. Empty holes looked straight down at the floor. His carpet looked new. It was stiff as if no one had walked on it yet. "How do I know it will shoot?" ... "You can trust me" ... "I'm not sure I can" ... "Why?" ... "I'm not sure I have a good answer for that" ... "Is it because I sell drugs?" ... "Could be" ... "There are a lot of worse people out there than drug dealers" he nodded to the group again. They shuffled their feet, exchanging glances. "It's okay. Look at the guy. He's got motherfucking pleated pants on. Do it." They all smirked. The short guy left around the corner. I heard a door open and shut. He came back into the living room with a box of bullets, setting it down next to the other two guns. "There's stacks of wood downstairs you can shoot into, if you really don't trust me." I latched the cylinder back into the frame and released it again. The small clinks of metal rose above our breathing. I set the gun down on the towel and opened the box of bullets. I pulled one bullet out at a time and lined them up on the glass, then picked up the revolver and dropped the bullets into the cylinder. I latched it into the frame. The bullets didn't alter the weight as much as I thought they were going to. "Gotta pull the hammer back" he scratched his chin. *Don't overthink it. Don't overthink. Hell, don't think about it just do it just do it,* and I gripped the handle, using my other hand to pull back the hammer, and held the gun up to the side of the short guy's head and squeezed the trigger. It took more pressure than I was hoping and the recoil punched my arm into the socket, sailing my hand over my head. I turned to the other two guys, and fired three shots hoping they'd get both of them. I couldn't tell because my eyes were closed.

11

Anything I wanted. "Sky's the limit," they said, following that statement with "pizza, burgers, nachos," as if those were the most exotic meals I could have come up with. But it's not like I blew their minds when I said medium-rare steak, baked potato with sour cream and bacon bits, and a Sprite. "Greens?" ... "Fuck, no!" The meal they brought on the beige plastic plate wasn't medium rare—not even close. It looked like they took a pilot torch and roasted the meat until it was well beyond caramelized. "This shit looks disgusting" ... "Steak" ... "I said 'medium-rare' steak" ... "You requested medium-rare. You'll eat what the chef makes you" ... "You sure a chef made this? I was thinking a mechanic" ... "My old man was a mechanic." I steeled myself and took three bites but couldn't finish. Potato— lumpy and cold in the middle. The skin was slimy and moist, a telling sign they didn't bake it for an hour but rolled it into a microwave for probably ten minutes—if that. I didn't even bother taking a bite, considering they didn't bring sour cream or bacon. I wasn't going to be hungry for long. I nodded to the guard and he threw it all away into the garbage can in the corner of the room. Plastic plate and all.

"She said you killed Frank, but I didn't believe her, to be honest. I did the normal, 'oh honey, I'm so sorry,' but between you and me—I figured he had finally left and she assumed the worst. That's what she does. Assume the worst" ... "You knew I was coming?" ... "I'm not stupid" ... "And them?" ... "They didn't know. I didn't want to worry them" ... "So they're clean of it all" ... "In a way" ... "Did you know my son?" ... "I know a lot of people" ... "My son is dead" ... "I know. It's been a few years, but yes, I knew your son. Tangentially."

49

The meth head's teeth were rotten—or in the process of rotting, which made them look pretty fucking rotten. It also made them weak. I didn't let the rotten-tooth-piece-of-shit say a word. I swung the mini bat. His teeth folded into his mouth. He staggered back, his hand reaching behind him for a wall to balance himself against, or a weapon. He could have been looking for a hidden-in-plain-sight weapon. I brought the bat up and down, conjuring images of a lumberjack chopping wood with a heavy ax, I aimed for his arm. After the snap and scream his hand swiveled, its mind disconnected from his own. "Is there anyone else here?" His eyes darted to the left. I swung again, bringing the tip of the bat down on the front of his shaved head. The skin split like I had used a knife, glossy white flesh exposed under the man's sixty-watt bulbs. It took seconds before the blood caught up to the wound, filling the crease with its crimson flow. He blinked and a thin stream cascaded down his forehead and around his nose. The meth head must have felt the blood coursing. He dropped to his knees, bringing his good hand to his face. Dabbing one finger into the blood, he held it out to examine it. It almost looked like a coming-to-Jesus moment. Before he had the opportunity to focus on anything else, I swung for the fences into his nose. The blood didn't hesitate for this one. It gushed not only from the nostrils but also from the crack on the bridge. He was choking on his words, doing his best to get them out of his throat. I placed my knee on the center of his Adam's apple and leaned my weight onto him. His arms flapped, and his disconnected hand flopped when the skin connecting it to the arm tugged it one way or the other. The bat made for messy work. I wasn't sure if I wanted it this messy, but it was going to have to do for the time being. After the meth head's body stopped vibrating, I took the stairs one at a time, looking for the other occupant.

15

I didn't feel the IV going in, but I knew the liquid was entering my vein. "Stop! I don't belong here. I know I've done some bad things. I know I'm not perfect. I know I'm a fuck up. But I didn't kill anyone." I pulled air into my lungs. I wanted to taste the air, but air has never had a taste. "I swear to God I didn't kill anyone and if that's the only reason you want to kill me then you are killing the wrong person." I wanted this air to be different. Noticeably different. I felt the tears roll down from my eyes. I squeezed my hands into fists and the broken finger screamed at the pain. I balled my fists tighter together against the straps. "Because I didn't kill anyone and I didn't kill anyone and I didn't kill anyone and I didn't kill your son, I didn't even know your son and I didn't kill him. Please please please don't kill me please. Is there anything? Can I say something that will make a difference" and the room dimmed to dark and every single man who's laid on this table probably said the exact

She asked what it was going to change. Was it worth losing the little bit of life I had left? Even if he was out there and I got him? What was that really going to do? She said the hate was a mental cancer hollowing me out. That's what she didn't understand. Knowing he was out there was its own kind of cancer draining me of everything I ever cared about. I wish I could say I didn't hate the man.

My phone said it was going to be a couple-hour walk. If I left then, I was going to show up way too early and create more suspicion by hanging around the neighborhood. Guys like this had watchers, or whatever the hell they wanted to call them. Kids, mostly, were their lookouts for suspicious characters and cops. If I was waiting around their block for four or five hours, the guy was going to know. So when I finally walked up to knock on the door, they were going to have their guns ready. I might not die, but I certainly wasn't going to get into the house. Instead, I walked halfway and stopped at a park. I sat down on a bench. I felt the bridge of my nose, and it was still too tender to explore with my fingers. It didn't look all that swollen in the mirror, but it was also covered in blood and bruises. After I saw my face, I didn't have any interest in looking at my chest. I should have gone home and slipped into bed next to Ness. Pretended none of this happened. I mean, not all of it. I can't pretend he's still alive. That's delusional. It's asking too much to act as if your son wasn't murdered, but I could pretend I accepted the murderer's death and continued on with my life, like Ness decided to. She was there. She had to know they put the wrong guy down, but she was still making a conscious effort to accept his punishment as truth. I could try. But would it stick? And when it came unstuck, was I still going to have these avenues available to me to pursue in attempt to get the guy? The real guy. The guy who actually killed my son. It's unlikely. Now was the time. Car doors slammed and kids came running through the wet grass. They climbed on the park's play structure, starting a game of chase or tag or some other imaginary game adults assumed was nonsense. Chances were that they were right. I probably wouldn't understand the game, but that's part of the charm. Enjoyment. The key. I used to bring him to the park on my days off. It was a way for him to burn off the energy acquired throughout the day, but it was also so I could see him interact with other kids. Was he going to be accepting and kind, or was he going to be aloof, or was he going to be outright mean? Kids don't have the filters and guards we're used to. They make friends in a matter of seconds, show their true feelings without much thought. The honesty of childhood is all at once appealing and horrifying. He ranged from one side of the spectrum to the other, and I was proud of him for it. He played chase and hide and seek and animals, giggling and laughing with strangers. When we left the park it was a tragedy—like I was tearing him away from his best friend and didn't care about the long-standing emotional trauma it was going to cause. Only a kid cares that much. It happened every time and it didn't matter how many times I said, "You have to have a good goodbye or we're not going to be coming back," we came back, and he always had a separation meltdown when we left. He grew up a little every year, and eventually, he was the one asking to leave, and then he was the one saying he didn't want to go to the park with me, and then he was saying he was too old, and he was the one sneaking out of the house to go to the park to smoke pot or drink beer or something else I didn't want to think about. I noticed the parents looking at me. My nose could have started swelling, or maybe I was out of place. I smiled at them and tucked my hands under my legs. I looked up at the sky hoping to see some birds flying, but it was blue skies. No clouds or anything.

20

This does not feel like it's over. This cannot be over. This is not over.

2

I never thought of myself as a bad person. I did what I needed to do, and sometimes did what I wanted to do, but I never thought any of it was bad. When I got older, vandalism became more appealing as a pastime, but even then, we targeted unbuilt houses. No one's life was necessarily getting wrecked by our destructive behaviors—just rich developers having to pay their guys a little more money while they backtracked to paint over the stupid cartoons we spray-painted on walls. Honestly, there was a good chance we never vandalized anything that wasn't already going to be covered up. And the graffiti—who was that hurting? We'd walk a mile into the woods to a water tank and spray paint some silly shit on there and suddenly we're a menace to society because people have a narrow idea of what is aesthetically pleasing? I guess when the drugs came along, I was harmful to others. I am sorry about that.

69

"You think you're on a mission, don't you?" ... "I wouldn't call it a mission" ... "Didn't Stubbs get put down?" ... "I don't know who Stubbs is" ... "Lethal injection. For killing that kid" ... "My son" ... "I've heard about your son. You are on a mission" ... "I wouldn't call it that" ... "Pops, here's the thing. Stubbs could have killed your kid" ... "He didn't"... "He didn't remember. At this point, none of us remember. You waited too long. Whatever you thought you saw doesn't mean shit. I'm not saying he did kill your kid, but I am saying he could've. Fuck, any one of us could have killed your kid."

72

Fingerprints. Blood. Whatever the hell else. Me. I was everywhere in the room, whether my breathing body was or not. I knew I needed to leave. I knew I was on borrowed time, and yet the seconds ticked away. I needed to sit down. I needed to sit down and close my eyes. If only for a few seconds. Tears brimmed along my lower eyelids, daring to drop over and cascade down my face. I just needed a few seconds, and I'd be okay. I just

Acknowledgments

I appreciate the deft and thoughtful readings from Ethan Wolcott and Paul Lee, who both helped me sharpen and hone this story.

Katie Emery, thank you not only for coming up with the phrase "Forever rage in our hearts," but for also allowing me to steal it for this book's dedication.

A big thanks to the Thirty West Publishing House crew, Josh Dale and Kat Giordano—I'm stoked to have this book be part of a such a rad press and appreciate the work you put into it. Additionally, I appreciate the hell out of Angelo Maneage and the absolute banger of a cover he designed (and all the concepts he originally presented us with).

And finally, Maureen Haeger, thank you for all the support anyone could even begin to dream of. I love you.

Bardo was written in the Buena Vista apartments, The Rocket Bakery on Cedar, and Iron Goat Brewing on 2nd while listening exclusively to The Front Bottoms' "Flashlight."

About the Author

Photo by Kelly Naumann

Joseph Edwin Haeger is the author of the experimental memoir *Learn to Swim* (University of Hell Press, 2015). His work has appeared in *Vol. 1 Brooklyn*, *Drunk Monkeys*, *HAD*, *X-R-A-Y*, and others. As a litmus test, he tells people his favorite movie is *Face/Off*, but a part of him is afraid that it's true. He lives in Spokane, WA with his family.

About the Publisher

Thirty West Publishing House

Handmade Chapbooks (and more) since 2015

www.thirtywestph.com / thirtywestph@gmail.com

Review our books on Amazon & Goodreads

@thirtywestph

Fall of Fiction 2023

Bardo by Joseph Edwin Haeger
(ISBN-13: 979-8-9861105-7-8)

Late Nights at Full Moon Records by Sarah Edmonds
(ISBN-13: 979-8-9861105-9-2)

Lizard People by Ryan Rivas
(ISBN-13: 979-8-9861105-8-5)

~

Fall of Fiction 2022

Broke Witch by Jessica Bonder
(ISBN-13: 979-8-9861105-3-0)

How to Keep Time by Kevin M. Kearney
(ISBN-13: 979-8-9861105-1-6)

Tentacles Numbing by Shome Dasgupta
(ISBN-13: 979-8-9861105-2-3)

www.ingramcontent.com/pod-product-compliance
Lightning Source LLC
LaVergne TN
LVHW040619250326
834688LV00035B/640